The Mysterious Dude of
Ghost Ranch

Stephanie St. Pierre

PRICE STERN SLOAN
Los Angeles

For Grandma and Grandpa St. Pierre

with love

Published by Price Stern Sloan, Inc.
11150 Olympic Boulevard, Suite 650
Los Angeles, California 90064
ISBN: 0-8431-2906-9
Printed in the United States of America
10 9 8 7 6 5 4 3 2 1

Contents

Way Out West

"Barbie!" shouted a happy voice. A tall girl waved from the porch. Her black braids flew out behind her as she ran down the steps. "I thought you'd never get here," she cried.

"Oh, Nia! It's great to see you," said Barbie. A soft breeze blew Barbie's hair around her face. It shone like gold in the bright sunshine. "I need a hat," Barbie said, pulling her hair back. "It's the one thing I forgot to bring." Nia looked at Barbie's two big suitcases and giggled. Barbie had just arrived at Ghost Ranch high in the Rocky Mountains.

"Let's hurry to your room," said Nia. "We can go for a ride after you change." She took one of the suitcases and led the way.

"It's really beautiful here," said Barbie. Across the driveway was a field where two chestnut horses ran through the grass. And beyond the horses, the mountains rose to high snowy peaks.

"You're going to love it," said Nia. Inside the ranch there was a large living room with a stone fireplace. As they passed the kitchen, they overheard a young man and woman arguing.

"Sometimes things get pretty crazy around here," Nia said. "But it's a lot of fun." They kept walking down a long hallway with lots of doors.

"Here it is," said Nia as she opened the door to a pretty bedroom. There was a brass bed with a colorful quilt. A vase of mountain wildflowers sat on top of an old dresser. In the corner stood an old-fashioned mirror.

"Oh, it's so nice!" said Barbie.

"I'll show you the stables later," Nia said. "I can't wait for you to meet Sun Runner. She's the most beautiful horse we've got, and gentle, too."

Barbie was really looking forward to this vacation with Nia. Two weeks of riding up into the mountains and helping out at the ranch seemed like a dream come true.

"There's just one more thing," Nia said. She opened the closet and took out a beautiful white cowboy hat. The headband was decorated with bright blue beads and colored feathers.

"Oh, Nia! It's perfect," said Barbie. "And it will look great with my new jacket."

"Hurry up and change now. I'll meet you back on the porch," said Nia.

Barbie quickly unpacked and changed out of the dress she was wearing. She slipped on a pair of jeans, a T-shirt and her pink cowboy boots. The jacket was hot pink with long fringe and had beautiful silver and blue needlework. She ran a brush through her wild hair and put on her new hat. Standing in front of the mirror she took in the new look.

"That will do fine," she said to herself. She looked like a rodeo queen! "Now to find Nia." Barbie headed for the front entrance. Just as she was passing the kitchen, she heard someone shout.

"Barbie! Barbie, come quickly!" It was Nia's voice. Barbie ran as fast as she could through the front door. As she came to the porch steps, she saw Nia and four of the ranch hands racing toward the stables. What could be the trouble?

2

Horse Trouble

"What's happening?" Barbie called. She caught up with Nia at the far end of the field.

"Something spooked the horses that were in the corral," Nia cried. She was out of breath from running. "And the gate is open. They've all run off. We've got to go after them." Nia pointed up a steep trail. Barbie was about to run, but Nia shook her head. "We'll never catch them on foot. Carl and Andy are bringing a couple of fast horses around." On cue the two ranch hands appeared. They were already on horseback and each one led another horse, saddled and ready to go.

"This is Sun Runner," said Nia. Sun Runner was a tall Palomino with a blond mane. Carl handed Barbie the reins. Then he took off up the trail with Andy.

"She's beautiful, all right," said Barbie. She pulled herself into the saddle and patted Sun Runner's neck.

"The other horses have a big lead on us," said Nia. She quickly climbed into the saddle of her horse. He was a shiny black stallion named Prancer. "Sorry you and Sun Runner didn't have more time to get to know one another," Nia said. "Ready?" Barbie nodded. Nia and Prancer hurried up the trail.

Barbie nudged Sun Runner with her heels and soon they were jogging up the trail after the others. They went as fast as they could but the trail was steep and narrow.

"The two chestnuts and a bay and her foal got out," Nia called to Barbie over her shoulder. When they reached a wider part of the trail she dropped back so they could talk. "We've got to find them before dark," Nia explained. "There are mountain lions up here, and with the foal, we can't be too careful."

"How far do you think they went?" Barbie asked. She couldn't help thinking about those lions.

"There's no way to know," said Nia. "But I think they'll probably head for the clearing near the waterfall. They like it there."

"What do you think scared them so?" wondered Barbie.

"I don't know," said Nia. She looked uneasy. "I was really hoping that nothing like this would happen while you were visiting." The trail narrowed again and the girls rode single file so Barbie couldn't ask Nia what she meant. They rode for a long time, hardly talking. The sun began to creep toward the mountains.

"We've probably got only another hour and a half before dark," said Nia. Just then Carl and his horse appeared on the trail heading toward them.

"We found them!" he shouted. When he got

closer he explained that Andy was waiting by the waterfall with the horses.

"Are they all right?" asked Barbie. Nia quickened her pace and rode ahead. Carl waited for Barbie to catch up with him.

"They're just fine," said Carl. "Strange thing is, somebody seems to have rounded them up."

"Who would do that?" Barbie asked.

"I don't know," answered Carl. "It wasn't horse thieves or they would have left someone watching." Carl scratched his head. "Too many strange things are going on around this ranch."

Barbie was going to ask what he meant when they came into a clearing. The trail ended at the waterfall. The horses were standing together, looking nervous, but okay. Andy had put bridles on all of them. He led the pretty bay foal to Barbie. The foal seemed calm and happily followed as Barbie walked over to join Nia.

"This is so strange," said Nia. "Someone

guided the horses over here and then trapped them in this corner." A pile of long logs and tree branches had been pushed aside, but Barbie could see how they had been used to keep the horses from leaving the far end of the clearing.

"Look here," cried Barbie. "There are some footprints." She bent down to look at the mud near the edge of the stream. "All of us are wearing cowboy boots. These look like prints from hiking shoes." She pointed to the funny pattern in the mud. The footprints crossed the stream and led toward the waterfall. In fact they seemed to disappear into it. "Should we follow them?" Barbie asked the others.

3

A Spooky Ride

Barbie stared at the place where the footprints seemed to vanish into the waterfall.

"No," said Nia, "I don't think we should follow those footprints now." Carl and Andy agreed. "Uncle Joe must be getting really worried," Nia said. The sun had sunk behind the snowy mountain peaks. It was getting dark in the clearing and on the trail, though the sky was still light. "And don't forget about the mountain lions," she added.

"I think we should get the horses back to the stables first, then try to figure out what happened," said Andy.

"I'm not sure whether I'm more worried about mountain lions or ghosts," said Carl.

Somehow the ride back down the mountain seemed spookier than the ride up had been.

Barbie could hear small animals rustling through the leaves in the dark woods on either side of the trail. Owls hooted. Far away a coyote howled and yipped. It got darker and darker.

It was getting windy too. Branches reached down and pulled at the riders' hats. Barbie couldn't help remembering Carl's remark. Had he been joking? Or did he really think the mountain was haunted?

Suddenly Prancer reared up and Nia screamed!

"What is it?" cried Barbie. "What's wrong?"

Nia got the horse under control. "It's okay," she said, looking scared. "I'm sorry. I thought I saw someone on the trail just ahead of me. So did Prancer, I guess." Nia patted the horse. "But it was nothing. Just a shadow, or a branch moving in the wind." Her voice sounded shaky. "Let's just get home."

Barbie was worried about her friend. Nia

seemed very upset. And she was feeling a little scared herself.

"Hey, does anybody know a good song we can sing?" Barbie said. "If we're loud enough I bet we can scare away anything in these woods."

"Good idea," said Carl. He and Andy knew a good cowboy song with lots of verses. They started singing, and soon Barbie and Nia joined in. The rest of the ride went more quickly.

"Yippee-i-a-kayo-o!" they sang as they finally reached the end of the trail. Everyone was glad when they saw the ranch lights blazing across the field. Someone was waving from the porch.

"It's Uncle Joe," cried Nia happily.

"Good work," said Uncle Joe as the gang led the tired horses into the stables. "You all get extra dessert tonight." He laughed merrily. "We'd all better get back to the house and wash up. Dinner's been ready for half an hour, and Aunt Julie hates to serve cold food." Uncle Joe, Barbie and Nia walked to the ranch house while Carl and Andy got water for the horses.

Alone in her room, Barbie thought about how strangely Nia and the ranch hands had acted. She left her coat and hat on the bed, washed up, brushed her hair and left her room.

Barbie met Nia just outside the door to the dining room. They hurried to the last two empty seats at the long table.

"Sorry I'm late," said Barbie, smiling at the pretty woman at the end of the table. She was sure that must be Nia's aunt Julie.

"Don't worry about it," Aunt Julie said with a welcoming smile. "We're all glad to have you here." Soon everyone's plate was piled high with fried chicken, biscuits and vegetables. For a while the only sound was the noise of silverware on plates. Finally the hungry group slowed down. Barbie was glad when the conversation began.

"What happened this afternoon?" asked a skinny man in a checked shirt.

"It seems as if Old Timer scared some of the horses," said Uncle Joe with a chuckle.

"I don't think it's so funny," said Aunt Julie. "So many odd things have been happening lately. I'm beginning to wonder about Old Timer." Nia and the ranch hands all nodded in agreement.

"Somebody—or some<u>thing</u>—did scare them, Uncle Joe," said Nia. "And no one saw anybody anywhere near there."

"Excuse me," said Barbie. "But who is Old Timer?"

"Why, didn't they tell you?" asked Uncle Joe. "He's the spook that haunts Ghost Ranch!"

4

Ghost Stories

"The spook that haunts Ghost Ranch!" said Barbie. "Are you sure there's <u>really</u> a spook?"

"I never thought there was a real ghost," said Nia. "But so many things have happened lately that just can't be explained—"

"I don't think it was a ghost that left those footprints up by the waterfall," said Barbie.

"But they <u>disappeared</u>," Nia said.

"We didn't get a very close look," said Barbie. "And it was getting dark."

"Why don't you go back up tomorrow and see what you can find out?" said Uncle Joe. "I'd like to know who it was that scared my horses."

"You can take a picnic and make a day of it," said Aunt Julie.

"And then you can take Barbie to Goldtown

Mine," added Andy.

"What's Goldtown Mine?" Barbie asked.

"I think you'd better tell her the whole story," Aunt Julie said to Uncle Joe.

"Oh, all right," said Uncle Joe. "But first I want to remind everyone that I don't believe a word of it. All this ghost business is just silly. Still, it does make a fine after-dinner story."

"Let's have dessert in the living room by the fire," said Nia.

"Good idea," said Uncle Joe. Everyone took their dishes to the kitchen. Nia introduced Barbie to Betsy, the cook, and Nick, her assistant. They were the same two people the girls had seen arguing earlier.

"I guess you two sorted things out," Nia said. Betsy and Nick looked puzzled for a minute, then realized what Nia was talking about.

"Oh, you heard us fighting," said Betsy with a smile. "I was mad at Nick for forgetting a box of groceries."

"I didn't," said Nick. He crossed his arms over his chest and glared at Betsy.

"Yes, I know," said Betsy, patting his arm. "I found the box later. It was already unpacked. All the cans and bottles were on the shelves. Everything was there except two cans of tuna fish. That seemed a little strange. But I never know what to expect these days." Betsy laughed.

"What do you mean?" asked Barbie.

"Well, things keep disappearing and then turning up in different places. Or other things just appear."

"Like what?" Barbie asked.

"Well, today I found a bowl of mountain berries in the refrigerator. It must have taken someone hours to pick them all. And when I asked who they belonged to, nobody knew," Betsy said.

"They must be ghost berries," said Nick. Barbie and Nia laughed. They each took a stack of dessert plates and left the kitchen.

Aunt Julie, Betsy and Nick brought in the desserts on a little cart.

"Dig in," said Aunt Julie. There was a chocolate cake and rice pudding and pecan pie—and the ghost berries and cream, of course. When everyone sat down, Uncle Joe began his story.

"It all started back in the year 1900," he said. "That was the year that United Metals came to the mountain. Back then, no one lived up here at all. It was just wilderness. United Metals sent a young fellow to look over the land, a prospector. Soon enough, he found gold and silver.

"Then the company sent more men to dig a mine. But nothing seemed to go right. First there was a long spell of heavy rain. Then everyone got the flu. Most of the men were too sick and weak to work.

"One night the young prospector was

checking the mine, to see how the beams were holding in all that rain. The beams fell on him. The other miners tried to rescue him, but when they cleared the rubble out, he was nowhere to be found. Legend has it that the mine just swallowed him up. People thought his ghost haunted the mountain. They started calling the ghost Old Timer."

Uncle Joe looked around at everyone. "Even though they say there's still silver and gold in the mine, no one wants to look. They say the ghost of Old Timer will bring the roof down on any man who tries to dig there."

Everyone sat staring into the fire, thinking about Old Timer.

"Wouldn't Old Timer haunt the mine instead of this ranch?" Barbie said.

"Maybe ghosts get lonely," said Nia.

"I don't know about that," said Uncle Joe. "I just thought it was kind of fun to tell guests the place was haunted."

"And then all these strange things started happening," said Aunt Julie.

"What has happened?" asked Barbie.

"There have always been stories about a man like a shadow up on the trails," said Nia.

"Then there's the horses bolting yesterday," suggested Carl.

"A lot of confusion in the kitchen," said Betsy.

"And—" One of the guests was about to add something when suddenly there was a big crash in the kitchen.

"What the blazes—" said Uncle Joe.

"My ghost trap!" said Nick. Everyone stared after him as he ran toward the kitchen.

5

On the Trail

"Let's go," said Barbie. She grabbed Nia's hand and hurried after Nick. "I want to get a good look at this ghost!" The girls found Nick staring at a mess of pots and pans on the floor near a wide-open window.

"Oh, my!" Barbie said, trying hard not to laugh. In the center of Nick's trap a small black-and-white cat was tangled in a net.

"Dexter!" Nick said, shaking his head and sighing. The cat looked up at him and meowed. Nick gently pulled the frightened cat from the net. Dexter shook himself off and ran to hide in the pantry.

"Nick," Nia asked. "How was this ghost trap of yours supposed to work?" Nick was blushing. The window was filled with pots and pans tied to pieces of twine.

"Well, I figured that if the ghost came through here he'd make a breeze that would rattle the pots and pans," Nick said. "And I also thought that if there wasn't a ghost and somebody was sneaking in here to play tricks on us, they'd get caught in that net and make a racket knocking over the pots."

"Poor kitty," said Barbie with a giggle. "Did you leave the window open?" she asked Nick.

"No," he said. "I'm sure it was closed."

"Well, somebody opened it," said Barbie. She peered out the window. "I don't see anything unusual out here, but it's pretty dark." She pulled her head back inside. "Let's look around out there in the morning."

"Okay," said Nia. "I definitely would rather hunt ghosts during daylight hours." They went back to the living room where everyone was talking excitedly.

"It was just Dexter," Nick said. "Sorry for all the noise."

"Well, I'm tired out," said Uncle Joe. "Good night." Soon Nia and Barbie were the only ones left sitting by the fire.

"We'd better get to sleep too," Nia said.

Barbie yawned. "You're right. I want to be ready for lots of riding and ghost-hunting tomorrow." The girls walked back to their rooms.

"Good night," Barbie said. She fell asleep as soon as she climbed into bed. All night long she dreamed of riding on the mountain, chasing a mysterious shadow.

At sunrise Barbie awoke, eager to start the day. She dressed in jeans, pink cowboy boots and a white blouse decorated with pink, green, yellow and blue flowers. Then she tied a pink ribbon around her ponytail and put on a pair of tiny silver earrings. "Ready," she said to Nia when her friend knocked on the door. She picked up her hat and pink jacket and followed Nia out the door.

"The weather doesn't seem too great," said Barbie. A fog had settled in around the ranch. It looked very spooky. "Do you think it's okay to go riding?"

"Oh sure," said Nia. "Once the sun's all the way up, the fog will just burn off. It's supposed to be nice, except for a thundershower later. But we should be home by then."

"I'm ready to go to the stables then," said Barbie.

"First things first," said Nia. "Aunt Julie made us pancakes and sausages."

"Mmm, my favorites," said Barbie. "And that reminds me, we need to check outside the kitchen window for footprints." She and Nia went to the kitchen. Barbie looked out the window. "Just as I thought," she said.

"What is it?" Nia asked.

"Don't those footprints look familiar?" Barbie pointed to a few marks in the mud by the window.

"Like the ones up at the waterfall!" said Nia.

The girls ate breakfast and then went out to get the horses ready. Uncle Joe came out to the porch just as they were about to leave.

"Here," he said. "Take this along." He handed Nia an old map of the mountain trails and the route to Goldtown Mine. "And be careful out there."

"We will be," said Nia.

"Maybe we'll even catch that ghost," said Barbie. Her blue eyes twinkled merrily. Aunt Julie joined Uncle Joe on the porch.

"Have fun," she called as the girls rode away. They crossed the field at a gallop. Barbie held on tight as Sun Runner almost flew. The horses seemed to be having as much fun as the girls were. Sun Runner was faster than Prancer.

"Ha! We beat you," Barbie said when Nia and Prancer caught up with them.

"Wait," Nia cried. Barbie was surprised to

see her friend looked worried. "I saw something," said Nia. "Or someone. I'm sure of it. It's so foggy, but I know it was a dark shape, going up the trail, fast."

"Then we'd better get after it in a hurry," said Barbie. She and Sun Runner were off like lightning. Nia didn't have any other choice but to follow.

6

The Mysterious Mine

As soon as Barbie got to the trail, she jumped off Sun Runner to look at the ground. Nia was right behind her.

"Well?" Nia asked. "What do you think?"

"I think these footprints are like the ones we saw by the waterfall and outside the kitchen," Barbie said.

Nia nodded. "I thought I saw a shadowy shape on the trail last night too ... just like now!"

"I think that shadow is your ghost," said Barbie. "Probably the same one who took the tuna fish from the kitchen yesterday."

"What does a ghost need with tuna fish?" asked Nia.

"I don't think it is a ghost, really," said Barbie. "I think that mysterious shadow is a person. And that person has been sneaking around pretending to be Old Timer."

"But why?" asked Nia. She was confused.

"I'm not sure yet," said Barbie. "Does your uncle Joe have any enemies? Can you think of anyone who might want to cause trouble on the ranch?"

"No," said Nia. "Everyone loves Uncle Joe."

"Then maybe it's somebody in trouble, somebody who needs help, food, a place to sleep, but is afraid to ask for it," said Barbie.

"But why would anybody be afraid to come to the ranch and just ask for help if they needed it?" Nia asked.

"I don't know," answered Barbie. "Let's go back to the waterfall and see if we can figure out where those footprints lead. Maybe we can track this <u>ghost</u> back to his hideout."

When they reached the waterfall, they were ready for a rest. The horses were thirsty and tired too.

"I can't get over how beautiful it is here," said Barbie as she sat watching the waterfall.

"Wait until you see the trees on the mountaintop," said Nia. "Some of them are thousands of years old. They're amazing."

"When can we see them?" Barbie asked.

"Not today," said Nia. "Not with a thunderstorm coming. It's a long hike. But we must see them before you leave."

"I can't wait," said Barbie. She walked toward the waterfall. The footprints were still there.

"There's no place to go from here but up," said Nia. She stood next to Barbie.

"Then that's where he must have gone," said Barbie. "Can we get up there?"

"I don't know," said Nia. "Let's look at the map Uncle Joe gave us." The girls spread the map out and read it carefully. "Here," said Nia. She pointed to a squiggly line. "It will take a long time. We'll have to backtrack the way we came first."

"Wait a second," said Barbie. "This trail also leads to the Goldtown Mine!"

"That's the mine that Old Timer is supposed to haunt!" said Nia with a shiver. "Maybe we <u>are</u> after a real ghost."

"I don't think so," said Barbie. "But somebody has gone to some trouble to make it seem that way."

It was afternoon when they reached the place they were looking for.

"I knew it!" Barbie cried. "Look at this." She pointed to more footprints in the mud near the edge of the cliff. "We've still got time to ride up to the mine, haven't we?" Barbie asked.

"What about the thunderstorm?" Nia reminded her.

"Well, I don't mind getting a little wet, do you?"

"No," said Nia. "It's getting too exciting to quit now." They rode on up the steep path.

Before long they saw the entrance to the old mine.

"There it is," cried Nia. "But look, someone has put up a <u>door</u>. How strange."

"Do you think someone lives there?" asked Barbie.

"There's only one way to find out," said Nia. The girls rode close to the mine and dismounted. They tied the horses to trees and knocked at the door. The only sound was the rumble of thunder far away.

"There's nobody here," Nia said. Barbie looked up and saw big black clouds rolling across the sky.

"Shall we go in and have a look around?" asked Barbie. "We may have to stay in there to get out of the rain—even if it is creepy."

"Okay," said Nia. "But let's be really careful." It was pitch-dark inside. Barbie turned on her flashlight.

"Oh my!" said Barbie. They were standing in

a living room! There was an armchair facing them. A painting hung on one of the walls. And against the other wall was a small stove.

"Look," said Nia. She shined her flashlight on two cans of tuna fish.

"The missing groceries!" Barbie cried.

"I wonder what's behind here?" said Nia. A blanket was hung across the tunnel behind the armchair. Nia disappeared behind the curtain.

Suddenly there was a loud clap of thunder, and Barbie dropped her flashlight. It went out as it hit the floor. As she reached for it, Barbie heard someone behind her. She spun around.

"Nia?" Barbie called. "Nia, is that you?!"

Lightning flashed across the sky. Someone was standing at the entrance to the mine, and it wasn't Nia.

"Old Timer!" Barbie gasped.

7

An Old Timer's Tale

Barbie was too scared to move. In another flash of lightning she saw the figure start toward her. Barbie took a step backward and crashed into something.

"Nia, it's—" Barbie was about to warn her friend to stay away when the room filled with light. Standing near the mine entrance was an old man, dripping wet, wearing a torn coat. There wasn't a ghost to be seen.

"You hurt, young lady?" asked the man. He held an oil lamp in one hand and a small bundle in the other. He put the bundle down on the table near his stove and hung the lantern on the wall. It filled the room with a warm yellow glow.

"Um, no," Barbie said. She almost felt like laughing. "I'm just fine."

"Got caught in the storm, did you?" asked the old man. He took off his coat and hung it on a root that stuck out of the tunnel wall. Nia appeared from behind the curtain.

"Oh!" she gasped. "Who are you?" The old man raised his eyebrows.

"I'm making tea," he said. "You can tell me what you're doing in my house while the water boils."

"Well," Barbie began, "we were looking for you, I guess." She noticed he was wearing old muddy hiking boots. "We thought maybe you might need help," said Barbie.

"Hmm," the old man looked thoughtful. "I don't need any help that I can think of."

"We wanted to thank you for corralling the horses," said Nia. "But you have to stop playing tricks on us at the ranch. It was you, wasn't it?"

"I'm not sure what you mean by tricks," said the man.

"You wanted us to think you're the ghost who haunts this mine, right?" said Barbie.

The old man sighed. "I'm not good at conversation," he said. "I've lived up here in the mountains almost all my life. I never bothered anyone. I don't want anyone bothering me now just because I've had a little hard luck." He opened his bundle full of leaves and roots and berries. The girls waited for him to go on talking, but he was quiet.

"But you didn't live here in the mine," said Nia. "It was all covered up."

"I used to live up a little higher, by the old trees. Had a much better view of things." Now the old man sounded angry. "Those darned developers pushed me out, bringing papers to prove I couldn't live there anymore. I've got my own papers, but I wasn't going to waste my time. I just packed up and left. I never liked being around people much."

"Developers?" Nia said. She was suddenly very worried.

"They came about two weeks ago," Old Timer said. "Finally got me so mad I just cleared out. I went back the next day and they'd torn down my house. Good thing I carried everything important away with me before that happened." He looked very sad.

"That's terrible," said Barbie. "Maybe we can do something to help."

"Everything's gone already," Old Timer said. He turned toward Nia. "I'm sorry if I scared anybody," he said. "I wasn't playing tricks. I didn't want to cause trouble. I didn't steal. I always left something to pay for what I took." The old man poured out three cups of tea.

"I didn't say you were stealing," said Nia. "But everyone thought the ranch was haunted. We thought you were the ghost from this mine."

"I'm no ghost," said the old man with a smile. "But I never stopped people from thinking I was one. That kept 'em away. I've heard that story too, about the mine falling on the gold prospector. There's plenty of truth in it." He chuckled. "But I'm not the ghost. My father is. I only wish those developers had known enough of that story to be frightened off." He looked sad again.

"You said you had some papers?" Barbie asked. "What did you mean?"

"Why, I'll show you," said Old Timer. He got out a tin box and placed it on the upside-down box that served as a coffee table.

"Wow!" said Nia. Inside the box there were old photographs and yellowed papers. Old Timer picked up a picture of a young man with slicked-down hair and funny old-fashioned clothes.

"That's my pa," said Old Timer. Barbie looked at the picture and then turned it around to see if there was a date or a name on the back.

"Oh my," she said. "I think we've found our

ghost after all! This is the miner that United Metals sent to survey the land." She pointed to a line of fancy script on the back of the picture.

"That part of the story is true," said Old Timer. "And he did die up here on the mountain. Maybe that's why I ended up living here."

"Oh, look," Barbie said. "It's stopped raining."

"Then I'll show you a shortcut to the ranch," said Old Timer. "If you don't get a move on, it'll be sunset before you know it."

"Just one thing," said Barbie. She picked up an important-looking paper from the box. "Can I take this if I promise to return it to you very soon?"

"I don't know..."

"I think this might be the key to getting those developers off the mountaintop," Barbie said.

"Well, if there's a chance of saving those old trees, why not?" Old Timer said. "So long as you promise to bring it back." Barbie promised. "All right then, let's get going." Old Timer led the way out of his strange home.

8

Mountaintop Mess

The girls found the horses a little nervous and wet, but okay. Soon Old Timer was leading them through the woods on a trail that neither one of them could have found without his help. There was no way they'd be able to find it again without him either.

"From here, you know the way," said Old Timer. He had led them to the exact spot where Prancer had reared up and Nia had seen the shadow.

"So it was you who scared my horse last night," Nia said.

"I'm sorry for scaring you, Miss," said Old Timer. "Now get on home."

"Could we bring you some supplies when we bring back the paper?" Barbie asked as he was about to turn to leave.

"Well," he said, "I'm mighty fond of tuna fish."

"Why don't you come to the ranch for dinner sometime?" said Nia.

"I like my privacy," said Old Timer. He turned and disappeared up the trail.

"What a strange man," said Nia.

"And a stranger story," said Barbie. "But he's very kind. I'm sorry he lost his house. But I think that paper I borrowed from him might show that he actually owns the land on the mountaintop."

"I'm worried about those developers," said Nia. "We've got to do something about them!"

"The first thing we do is tell Uncle Joe and everyone else on the ranch about this," said Barbie. "Next we've got to find out where the developers are and what they're doing. Then we can go into town and find out who really owns the land. We need to show this paper to somebody who can tell if it's worth anything."

When Uncle Joe heard Barbie and Nia's tale, he was very upset.

"The county is not supposed to sell mountain land without a town meeting," he cried. "I'd like to know how those developers got around that rule."

"We're going up tomorrow to find out what they're doing," said Barbie. "Then we'll check the records at town hall."

"We'll find out why there wasn't a town meeting too," said Nia. Everyone was ready to take action if the developers had plans to hurt the area.

No one slept well that night. When morning finally came, the whole ranch was up earlier than usual. Everyone wanted to help.

"I think you girls should have some company if you're going all the way up the mountain. It's a long ride, and those developers might be unfriendly," Carl said. Andy had already saddled the horses and they were ready to go.

"Okay," said Barbie. "We can sing some more cowboy songs. If they scared away wild animals, then maybe they'll scare away mean developers." Everyone laughed.

"Let's get going!" Nia said. Because they were in a hurry, they took the bridle path that followed the road up the mountain. The horses galloped full speed. Barbie loved the way the wind felt, blowing her hair out behind her. She hugged tight to Sun Runner as the horse raced ahead of the others.

It was a very long ride. They stopped to let the horses rest and take a short lunch break.

"Do you have any idea where we should look?" Barbie asked Nia and the guys.

"I think I've seen the shack the old man told you about," said Andy. "I could take us there."

"That sounds like the best place to start," said Nia.

"Then we'd better ride on," said Barbie. She smoothed Sun Runner's long golden mane and patted her. "Good horse," she said. "Tomorrow I promise to braid your hair and cover you with ribbons. Now giddy-up!" The horse took off, glad of the chance to go as fast as she liked.

They had been riding hard and long. Everyone was getting tired. But they knew they were on the right track when they saw the KEEP OUT sign.

"They've been back here with cars and trucks," Carl said, looking at the road. Finally they found what they were looking for.

"Oh, no," Nia said as they came around a bend. Her eyes filled with tears. The trail had suddenly ended, opening onto a bald patch on the mountain. A bulldozer was shoving fallen trees over the side of a cliff. Two men were looking at some papers.

"They've cut down all the beautiful old trees!" cried Nia.

9

A Dirty Deed

"Wow!" Barbie said. The trees were amazing. They were twisted and bent into odd shapes. Their trunks were so old they looked dead, but deep green needles burst out in clumps at the end of the branches. Most of the land was still covered with that unusual forest, but the large bald patch was growing as the bulldozer pushed its way along.

"The poor trees!" Nia cried. "Oh, dear. They'll ruin everything! Barbie, what are we going to do?"

"Don't worry. We'll find a way to stop them," Barbie said. "Let's get out of here." They were turning around when the men looked up and saw them. The men started shouting. "Let's go!" Barbie and Sun Runner led the way. If they could have ridden home any faster they would have. It was more important than ever that they get to town today, before too many more trees were destroyed. But the horses had to stop to rest a few times.

"I'm so mad, I want to scream," said Nia. She watched as Prancer drank from a stream. His coat glistened with sweat. "The horses are getting really tired."

"I know," said Barbie. "We're going to have to slow down."

"We'll still make it into town before it's too late," Carl said. They were about to mount when a pickup truck suddenly came to a screeching stop in the road beside them.

"What did you think you were doing, nosing around on private property?" asked the driver.

"We were just out for a ride," said Barbie sweetly. "We didn't know anybody was up there."

"I'll bet you didn't," said the driver. "Take my advice and stay far away from there." He glared at them and then drove away.

"I really don't like him," said Nia. No one could disagree.

The rest of the ride seemed to take forever. When they reached the ranch, Barbie and Nia ran to find Uncle Joe.

"We're ready to go into town now," said Barbie. They told him what they had found.

Uncle Joe had called the mayor already and asked him to meet them at town hall. Barbie and Nia changed into fresh clothes and met Uncle Joe in the car.

"You look beautiful," Nia said. Barbie was wearing a purple dress, purple shoes, a silver necklace and silver earrings. She'd brushed her hair out like a golden cloud around her shoulders.

"This is my going-into-town outfit," said Barbie. "Everything else is too casual. Besides, you know I love to dress up." As they sped along in the car toward town, the girls and

Uncle Joe discussed their plan to get rid of the developers. They were all excited when they reached town hall.

The mayor was as worried about the mountaintop as everyone else. They all stood in the musty basement looking through a fat file of papers.

"Do the developers own that land?" Barbie asked. The mayor looked through the pile until he found a bill of sale for the land.

"Well," he said, holding up the paper, "I'm afraid they did buy the land, fair and square from the county."

"But it belongs to Old Timer," said Barbie.

"Who?" asked the mayor. Barbie and Nia told the mayor the story of the old man who lived on the mountain

"You mean there's a real Old Timer living up there?" the mayor asked. "He'll have to prove he is who he says he is, and show us a deed."

"I've got the deed here," said Barbie. She

held out the old paper. The mayor read it carefully.

"This means he still owns all that land—unless he sold it to the county."

They all helped to look through the papers. It took a long time, but finally they finished.

"There is no record here of that land ever being sold by your friend, Old Timer. The county made a mistake in selling the land to the developers," said the mayor.

"Hurrah!" Nia and Barbie shouted.

"Wait a second," said the mayor. "You'll have to get Old Timer to come out of the woods and prove who he is."

"Oh, he'll do it," said Barbie. "He wants to save those trees as much as any of us."

"We'll meet at the ranch tomorrow morning with a group of people," said the mayor. "Even if your friend doesn't come, we can make the developers show their plans to the town."

"We'll have to call everybody on the

mountain and in town," Barbie said, "to be sure they show up at the meeting." If only they could call Old Timer. He was the only person who could solve this problem once and for all. Maybe he would show up on his own. After all, he'd been keeping a pretty close eye on the ranch.

10

Showdown

"Is everything ready?" asked Uncle Joe. He was nervous about the meeting.

"I hope we get a good crowd," said Aunt Julie.

"Well, we should," said Nia. "We called more than two hundred people last night."

First the mayor arrived. Soon dozens of people were wandering around the yard.

A stand with a microphone was set up on the porch. The mayor stood up and began to speak. Suddenly he was interrupted.

"We bought that land and have the right to work up there," said a gruff voice. It was one of the developers. "Who are you to tell us what to do with it?"

"You can't destroy the wilderness on our mountain," Uncle Joe cried.

"You can't pollute our rivers and streams," yelled Nia.

"Or drive out the wild animals," added Barbie.

"It's our land," the man said again. "And we'll keep you off it, and we'll go on with our business whether you like it or not." Before long everyone was shouting. Things were getting out of hand.

"Hold on," said a calm voice over the microphone. It was Barbie. "There's one important fact—"

"You're just a troublemaker," yelled the developer. "In a few days it will be too late for any of you to complain. Nothing you have to say can change that."

"You're wrong," Barbie began, "because ..." She stopped. He was there in the crowd. She had seen that dark shadowy shape. "...because that land really belongs to someone else."

"What are you talking about?" said the developer.

"I'm talking about the man who lived on that land all his life, and took care of it," she said. "I know that once he understands what you're doing up there, he'll call a stop to it."

"You mean that crazy old guy?" The developer started to laugh. "He didn't own that land! He didn't own anything."

"He did," Barbie said. "He inherited it from his father who made the first claim on that land back in 1900. Everyone who lives here knows him," Barbie said. "Though most of you probably thought he was a...well...a ghost."

A whisper went through the crowd. Suddenly a dark shape appeared behind Barbie on the porch.

"I'm not a ghost," said the old man. He moved toward the stand as Barbie stepped away. "I've been living on my own and happy that way. I would've gone on doing that except for these fool developers running down my house with their machines." He glared out at the developer in the crowd.

"Go away, you old man," yelled the developer. "You were on <u>our</u> property."

"You're wrong about that." The mayor had stepped up to the microphone. He held an old paper over his head. "This is the deed to the land on top of the mountain. It clearly says that this man," the mayor pointed to Old Timer, "is the owner of the mountaintop and the old mine."

The crowd began cheering. The developer was red in the face. He pushed his way to the mayor and demanded to see the deed.

"It can't be real," he said.

"Oh, it is," said Barbie. "I guess you're the one who has broken the law."

The mayor turned to Old Timer. "We'll do what we can to rebuild your house."

"No, no," said Old Timer. "I've got a new house I like fine. I just want my privacy." He was smiling. "I'll tell you what though. I've decided that I wouldn't mind having a little company sometimes. I might invite you up to the mine for tea." The mayor looked surprised.

"I'll be getting home now," said Old Timer. He started to leave and then stopped.

"Thank you, young ladies," he said to Barbie and Nia. "I don't mind losing one house so much, but I'm mighty glad you showed me how I could save those beautiful old trees." The girls watched as Old Timer disappeared into the crowd. Soon everyone was gone.

"That was a great meeting," said Nia. She and Barbie were sitting alone on the porch.

"You can say that again," said Barbie. "It's been a great week!"

"Maybe we should just sit here for the rest of your visit," Nia said, laughing.

"That sounds good," said Barbie.

"Oh, Barbie," called Aunt Julie. "There's a phone call for you." Barbie ran inside and grabbed the phone. It was Christie!

"I have a big favor to ask," Christie said. "It

couldn't wait till you got home."

"Well?"

"Children's Charities is having a Dance-a-thon to raise money this year. I'm in charge of it," Christie said.

"That's terrific," said Barbie. "What can I do to help?"

"You can pick all the bands and the food and perform and plan the decorations," said Christie.

"Fantastic!" said Barbie. "Are you sure you want me?" It sounded like a fun project. And Barbie loved anything to do with dancing!

"There's nobody I can think of who'd do a better job," said Christie. "We've got exactly four weeks to plan everything. Oh, please say you'll do it."

"Okay, I will," said Barbie. "I'll call you when I get home."

"Barbie, you're the best!" said Christie.